ThunderTrucks! is published by Stone Arch Books
a Capstone imprint
1710 Roe Crest Drive
North Mankato, Minnesota 56003
www.mycapstone.com

Cataloging-in-Publication Data is available on the
Library of Congress website.

ISBN: 978-1-4965-5737-7 (library hardcover)
ISBN: 978-1-4965-5741-4 (eBook)

Summary: The PERSEUS monster truck soars over
ginormous jumps and takes on his enemy, MEDUSA!

Designed by Brann Garvey

Printed in Canada
010797S18

THUNDERTRUCKS!

GAS GUZZLER!

BY BLAKE HOENA

ILLUSTRATED BY FERN CANO

STONE ARCH BOOKS
a capstone imprint

CONTENTS

CHAPTER ONE

BROKEN DOWN

*Putt-putt-putt-*BANG!

*Putt-putt-putt-*BANG!

A run-down pickup truck sputters

back and forth in front of a repair shop.

Suddenly, the garage door opens. Out

rolls the shop's owner, a rough-looking

tow truck with a large, dangling winch.

"What's all the racket?" he honks.

"Sorry, Poly-D!" sputters the truck.

Putt-putt-putt-BANG!

"What do you need this time,

Perseus?" the owner asks, annoyed.

"What don't I need?" replies the

pickup. "A new transmission, muffler,

mud flaps, rearview mirrors–"

"Your shocks look pretty good," Poly-D interrupts.

"If I'm gonna remain an official ThunderTruck, I need to do more than jump," Perseus explains.

"I'm sure there's something else you can do," says the owner. "Just think about it."

Perseus shakes his hood.

"Well," adds Poly-D, "all those repairs will cost you."

"But I've been running on empty for months," Perseus beeps sadly.

Poly-D shrugs his fenders, and Perseus's front grill bends into a frown.

Just then, Perseus spots something in his headlights. A flyer for the **World Endur-X Championship**

hangs on a wall of the shop.

It is the longest, and possibly the most dangerous, race ever.

Competitors start in the city of Trolympia. They race over a towering mountain, across a bottomless bog, and through an endless desert to the end of the world — and back again.

The flyer says the winner will receive

free repairs for a year!
"I will be back!" Perseus

says, determined.

Putt-putt-putt- **BANG!**

CHAPTER TWO
THE ENDUR-X CHAMPIONSHIP

The next day, Perseus sputters into Trolympia.

*Putt-putt-putt-***BANG!**

The city's rocky streets are already crowded with fully fueled race fans. They wave colorful banners in support of their favorite ThunderTrucks.

"HERCULES!
     HERCULES!"

Some trucks honk.

"B-PHON! B-PHON!"

Others beep.

Perseus follows the other trucks toward the Endur-X Championship starting line.

"HONK!" A race official suddenly blares at the pickup truck. "Only fully repaired ThunderTrucks are allowed in this race."

Perseus believes his plan has already backfired. Just then, the sellout crowd revs with excitement.

"ARGONUTZ! ARGONUTZ!"

Perseus spins on his wheels and spots Argonutz 'N Bolts. The popular ThunderTruck's golden fenders sparkle in the sunlight.

Behind him, an evil monster truck slowly approaches. Puffs of gray smoke billow from her dent-covered hood. She is a real rust bucket!

"Who's that?" Perseus asks the security guard.

CRUNNNNNCH!

The mysterious monster truck suddenly slams into Argonutz's rear bumper.

THUNK!

His golden fenders instantly crash to the ground, and the ThunderTruck stalls before reaching the starting line.

The official shifts into high gear. *"Medusa!"* he exclaims, rattling with fear. "Best stay away from her! She's a real gas guzzler!"

"What do you mean?" Perseus asks.

"One fender bender with her could **suck** the life out of anytruck!" he says. Then *ZOOOOOM!*

The official puts pedal to metal and speeds off.

Perseus thinks about doing the same, but he knows this is his only shot at entering the race.

*Putt-putt-putt-***BANG!**

He sputters up to the starting line.

"I didn't know you were coming," another truck asks him. It is Theseus, the first to conquer the Monster Maze.

"I . . . um . . . Argonutz couldn't make it," Perseus tells him. "I'm taking his place."

"Just don't think you're going to beat me!" Atalanta blares from her position at the starting line. Everytruck knows she's the fastest truck in the world!

Looking down the starting line,

Perseus also spots Hercules and B-Phon.

He sees a giant truck called Bullistic and

another known as Hydra. Then there's

Cyclops, a truck with only one headlight,

and a mean-looking truck

called The Boar.

Ten racers in all.

Perseus thinks he

doesn't stand a chance!

Moments later —

Baaaaawoooogaaahhh! — a loud

horn blows. The race official returns.

"Racers take your mark," he sputters,

keeping a close headlight on Medusa.

"Get set . . ."

VROOOOOOM!

Engines roar.

RUMMBLE!

The ground shakes.

Everytruck cheers.

"Go!" the official declares.

Knobby tires spin on the gravel, and

the trucks dart forward.

CRUNNNNNCH!

Before the trucks even reach second

gear, Medusa rams Cyclops! His lone

headlight cracks and falls to the ground.

Then — **POOF!** — a puff of smoke

billows out from under his hood.

Seconds later, **SMAAAASH!** Medusa crashes into B-Phon, and his tires instantly go flat.

"Hey!" B-phon says too late. "No fair!"

Just like that, the race is down to eight trucks!

CHAPTER THREE

MOUNTAIN MADNESS

Perseus speeds past the broken-down
Cyclops and B-phon. All around him,
row upon row of trucks line the
Endur-X Championship course.

Through the crowd, Perseus
spots the towering Mount Trolympus
in the distance. It will be their first
big obstacle!

Suddenly, a giant, flame-red monster truck steers toward Perseus.

Thick, black smoke spews from two horn-shaped pipes on the vehicle's hood. Bullistic is headed straight for him!

WHAM-O!

Before he can reach Perseus, Medusa slams into Bullistic. His flame-red paint job instantly rusts, and his engine stalls.

Then Medusa turns her evil headlights on Atalanta. The World's Fastest Truck tries to get out of the way. But Medusa rams into Atalanta's side.

SMAAAAASH!

Suddenly, all four of Atalanta's tires fly off and roll away. THUD!

Her body lands on the dirt and smoke pours out from under her hood.

A nervous air bubble builds in Perseus' gas line. "Only six racers left," he gulps.

Mount Trolympus rises in front of Perseus. Some of the other racers have already reached its base. They zoom up a winding canyon that leads toward the top. Perseus follows in their dusty tire tracks.

As he speeds along, two large shadows suddenly cross his path. Then he hears a loud **BOOM** and feels the ground shake and rumble.

Ahead, on the path, a large boulder tumbles down the mountainside.

CRASH!

BANG!

BOOM!

It rolls back and forth down the path.

As it nears Perseus, he spots small pile of rocks off to the side. He races over to them and leaps into the air.

Perseus sails safely over the boulder
as it crashes down the hill.

Where did that come from? he thinks.

A little farther up the mountain,
Perseus sees Hydra. One side of the
canyon wall has collapsed on him. The
evil truck is buried under a pile of dirt
and rocks!

"What happened?" Perseus asks.

"I don't know," Hydra rumbles. "A boulder just fell out of the sky!"

"Do you need help?" Perseus asks.

"NO!" Hydra growls. "Not from a beat-up ThunderTruck!"

Perseus races away, but he looks back to make sure Hydra gets out okay.

He sees Medusa racing up to Hydra.

Hydra is still pinned under the rocks when Medusa rams into him.

Hydra's tires stop spinning, and his engine starts to *wheeze* and *cough*. Then his headlights flicker and dim.

Medusa keeps chugging up the mountain.

Only five racers remain — and Medusa is right on Perseus's mud flaps!

CHAPTER FOUR

THE GORGONATERS!

When Perseus reaches the top of Mount Trolympus, he sees the other racers. Medusa chugs up the mountain behind him. Ahead of him, Hercules, Theseus, and The Boar speed down the other side of the mountain.

With his jumping ability, Perseus

hopes he can catch up to them. He races

over a small berm and leaps into the air.
FWOOOSH!

He soars part way down the mountain.

Then he races over a larger berm —

FWOOOSH! — and he sails even

farther down!

Perseus catches up to the other

racers at the bottom of the mountain.

But he only sees Hercules and The Boar.

They are stopped in the middle of

the road.

Perseus rolls up to them.

"What's wrong?" he sputters.

"Sometruck dug a pit in the middle of

the track," The Boar rumbles.

In front of them, there is a large hole.

At the bottom of it is Theseus!

"Are you okay?" Hercules yells down to him.

"Think I have a sprained axle," Theseus blares. "You'll have to go on without me."

Now only four racers remain!

"What do we do?" Perseus asks.

Just then, a familiar sputtering and chugging comes from behind him. They all turn to see Medusa.

"Let's get out of here!"

Hercules honks.

The ThunderTruck climbs over some boulders on the side of the pit. The Boar tries to follow, but the rocks shift under the gigantic truck's weight.

Perseus is not much of a climber. He is a jumper. He backs up to get a running start. His engine revs, his tires spin, and then he takes off. As he nears the edge of the pit, he leaps into the air.

Perseus soars over the pit and lands with a **THUMP** on the other side.

He stops to look back. Hercules is almost past the pit. But The Boar is stuck on the other side.

Medusa rolls up to him and gives him a nudge. All of The Boar's doors fall off. His lights flicker. Then his engine *hiccups* and coughs a puff of smoke.

"Get going!" Hercules shouts to Perseus.

With only three racers left, Perseus takes the lead!

Up ahead, Perseus discovers the next obstacle — a bubbling and oily bog!

Through the bog lies a twisty dirt path.

Perseus glances back to see if Hercules is following him. What he sees frightens him. As Hercules speeds around one twist in the path, a dark shadow swoops down. It rams into him. **KA-BLAM!** Hercules almost slides off the path!

Then as Hercules races around a curve, another dark shadow dives down. It crashes into Hercules, and he flies off the path. With a *SPLOOSH*, he lands in the bubbling oil and is stuck.

Now the race is down to just Perseus and Medusa!

On the other side of the bog lies the final obstacle — endless desert! Sandy dunes stretch out as far as he can see.

Perseus stops to take a break. He looks back and sees the large, shadowy shapes towing Medusa across bog. They set her down on the other side.

"Who are they?" Perseus asks.

"The Gorgonaters!" Medusa blares. "These monster trucks are exactly like me — with one upgrade. They can jump even higher than you!"

"We dropped that boulder on Hydra," one Gorgonater rumbles.

"We dug the pit that trapped Theseus," the other grumbles.

"And now we will get you!" they squeal together.

Perseus takes off! His tires spin in the loose sand.

Putt-putt-putt-**BANG!**

Putt-putt-putt-**BANG!**

Putt-putt-putt-**BANG!**

He cannot go very fast, and the Gorgonaters are right behind him.

Up ahead, Perseus spots a large dune, and a smile spreads across his grill. He has an idea!

Perseus speeds up it — faster and
faster — forcing the Gorgonaters to
follow. "It's not how high you can jump—"
he honks back at the evil trucks.

FWOOOOOOOSH!

He soars off the dune like a ramp, and the Gorgonaters do the same.

Perseus lands safely on the other side. "It's how well you land on your wheels," he finishes.

CRASH!

WHOOOOMP!!

The Gorgonaters spiral out of control and land engine-deep in the sand.

"NOOOOOOOO!" Medusa cries. Only she and Perseus remain.

CHAPTER FIVE

BEYOND REPAIR

As Perseus speeds through the desert, grayness surrounds him. The path narrows, and the ground drops away on either side. He races along a thinning ledge until the land ends at a narrow point. He has reached the end of the world.

Perseus rolls up the edge of the cliff and peers down.

There is only grayness below and only grayness ahead. He is surrounded by grayness, except for the path he just drove down.

"I've got you now,"

Medusa rattles.

Perseus spins around.

Medusa blocks his path.

Perseus knows he cannot let her touch him. But there is no way around her. And the path here is flat. He does not have even the tiniest of bumps to use to leap over her.

But Perseus has an idea. Medusa is always chasing after other trucks, and they are always running away scared. Maybe he needs to give *her* a scare.

Perseus revs his engine. He spins his tires, kicking up a cloud of dust.

"What . . . are . . . you . . . doing?" Medusa gasps.

"I'm going to ram you off the path," he honks.

Then Perseus screeches toward her. Medusa's headlights flicker in fear. She backs away.

As she does, one of her tires slips off the narrow ledge. It *whirs* and it spins in the air.

Perseus now has just enough room to get by her. He swerves around her, with his tires on the edge of the ledge.

He races by her and speeds back through the endless desert. He weaves around the twisty and curvy path through the bottomless bog. He climbs up and over the towering Mount Trolympus.

Then he races through the streets of Trolympia and back into the arena. Fans honk as he crosses the finishes line.

"And the winner is," the race official shouts in disbelief, **"Perseus!"**
*Putt-putt-putt-**BANG!***

After receiving his prize, Perseus returns to Poly-D's Repair & Salvage Shop. What he finds there surprises him!

Several trucks are outside. There is Jason with his fender attached, and B-phon has a new bumper. Atalanta, Hercules, and Theseus are also fixed.

Off to the side are the evil monster trucks — all of them except for Medusa. They are testing out their new repairs.

Perseus rolls up to the garage. He sees Poly-D working on a beat-up truck up on the lift. Then Perseus recognizes who is up on the lift.

Medusa!

"Stay away from her!" Perseus warns.

"Why? Medusa's my best customer," Poly-D says. "It could take days . . . weeks . . . maybe years to fix everything wrong with her."

Perseus rolls back outside. He is joined by all the ThunderTrucks.

"What are you doing here anyway?" Theseus asks. "You won the race."

"Exactly," Perseus replies. "I'm using the prize to finally get the repairs I need."

"You're beyond repair!" Hercules says.

Perseus's grill folds into a frown. He'll never remain an official ThunderTruck, he thinks.

Then B-Phon says, "He means, you can't fix what isn't broken."

"Really?" Perseus's headlights beam brightly.

The others rev their engines. "Once a ThunderTruck, always a ThunderTruck!" they say.

Putt-putt-putt-BANG!

PERSEUS AND MEDUSA

Gas Guzzler! is based on the Greek myth of Perseus and the Medusa.

Perseus was a famous Greek hero. His father was Zeus, god of the sky. His mother was Princess Danaë.

King Polydectes ruled the island where Perseus and his mother lived. The king threatened Perseus' mother. To save her, Polydectes ordered him to slay Medusa.

Medusa was a horrible monster with snakes for hair. She was so frightening that anyone who gazed into her eyes was turned to stone. King Polydectes really hoped that Medusa would turn Perseus to stone.

But Perseus had help on his quest. Hermes, messenger of the gods, gave him winged sandals so that he could fly. Athena, goddess of wisdom, gave him a sword and a bronze shield.

Perseus traveled to the ends of the world to battle Medusa. He couldn't look at the horrible monster, or he would be turned to stone. So Perseus used Athena's shield as a mirror to find Medusa. Then he cut off her head.

Perseus returned to Sisyphus with Medusa's head. He showed it to Polydectes and turned the king to stone. His mother was saved!

BLAKE HOENA

Blake Hoena grew up in central Wisconsin, where he wrote stories about robots conquering the moon and trolls lumbering around the woods behind his parents house. He now lives in St. Paul, Minnesota, with his wife, two kids, a dog, and a couple of cats. Blake continues to make up stories about things like space aliens and superheroes, and he has written more than 70 chapter books and graphic novels for children.

FERN CANO

Fernando Cano is an illustrator born in Mexico City, Mexico. He currently resides in Monterrey, Mexico, where he works as a full-time illustrator and colorist at Graphikslava Studio. He has done illustration work for Marvel, DC Comics, and role-playing games like Pathfinder from Paizo Publishing. In his spare time, he enjoys hanging out with friends, singing, rowing, and drawing.

GLOSSARY

bog (BOG) — an area of wet, spongy land

canyon (KAN-yuhn) — a deep, narrow river valley with steep sides

competitor (kuhm-PET-i-tur) — one that competes against another in a contest

fender (FEN-dur) — a protective guard over a wheel of an automobile, motorcycle, or bicycle

muffler (MUHF-lur) — a device that reduces the noise made by an engine

racket (RAK-it) — a very loud noise

transmission (transs-MISH-uhn) — a series of gears that send power from the engine of a vehicle to the wheels

winch (WINCH) — a machine that has a roller on which a rope, cable, or chain is wound for pulling or lifting

READ MORE
HIGH-OCTANE ADVENTURES!

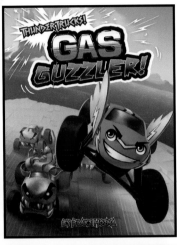

ONLY FROM
CAPSTONE